GW01319833

Bella and Bertie's Antics in Ancient Egypt

Written by
Cindy Whitbread

Illustrated by
Corrina Holyoake

Bella and Bertie's
Antics in Ancient Egypt

Cindy Whitbread
Text & images © Cindy Whitbread

All rights reserved. No part of this publication
may be reproduced, stored in any retrieval
system or transmitted in any form or by any
means, electronic, mechanical, photocopying,
recording or otherwise, without the prior
written permission of the copyright holder
for which application should be addressed in
the first instance to the publishers. The views
expressed herein are those of the author
and do not necessarily reflect the opinion
or policy of Tricorn Books or the employing
organisation, unless specifically stated. No
liability shall be attached to the author, the
copyright holder or the publishers for loss or
damage of any nature suffered as a result of
the reliance on the reproduction of any of
the contents of this publication or any
errors or omissions in the contents.

ISBN 9781912821280

A CIP catalogue record for this book
is available from the British Library.
Published 2019 Tricorn Books
131 High Street, Portsmouth, PO1 2HW

Printed & bound in the UK

Bella and Bertie's

Antics in Ancient Egypt

YES!

WRITTEN BY
CINDY WHITBREAD
ILLUSTRATED BY CORRINA HOLYOAKE

It was a blusterous, gusterous, dusterous day.

But, Bella and Bertie needed to play.

While the wind and rain rampaged through the sky and the trees,

the thought of darting through time never failed to please.

"Let's go and be silly with Sabre Tooth Tilly."
"No, Bella, she's going to the dentist's today, silly."

"What about cool-as-school Lucas, in the African sun?"

"Nope, he's having his mane washed before he goes for a run."

"Let's somersault with Mason in the Moon today…..."
"No, ninny he's eating cheese and beans with Rosie May."

"I know! Let's gust through the dust of the soft silky desert."
"Yes! We can spring, swing and schwing with Ancient Egypt Egbert."

"Bella, do you have your feather, weather header?"

"Yep. Have you found your blether, whatsibrella?"

"Yes, and ready to go… but my tummy's full of funny mumbles."

"Ha, ha, that's okay, mine's got belly bubble-making rumbles."

Bertie's eyes flashed with a command so grand.

Bella's eyes blasted them towards their adventure land.

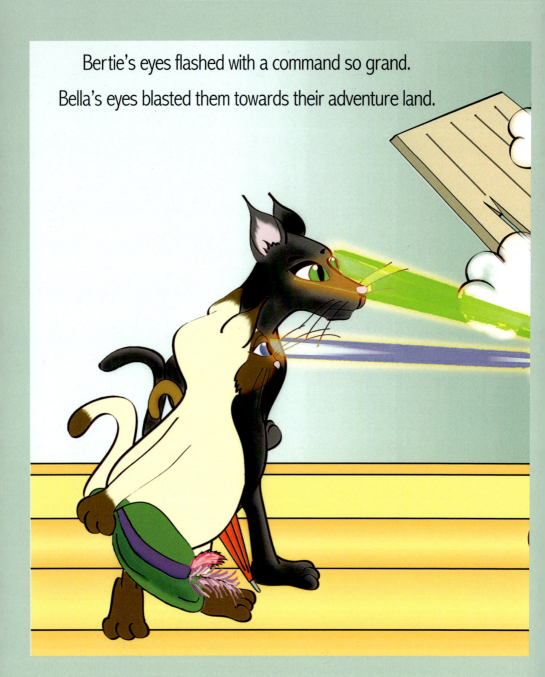

"WHAAHOO! We're flying like superheroes and stars."
"Look," said Bella, "there's Jupiter and Mars."

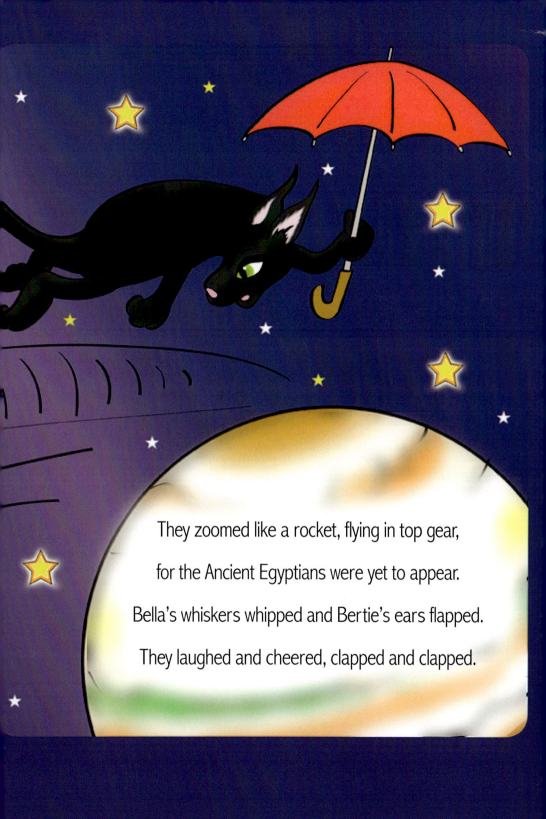

They zoomed like a rocket, flying in top gear,

for the Ancient Egyptians were yet to appear.

Bella's whiskers whipped and Bertie's ears flapped.

They laughed and cheered, clapped and clapped.

They marvelled and swooned at many magnificent sights,

from dinosaurs, to castles and friendly-looking knights.

Suddenly they saw a place so wondrous and striking,
they forgot to plan an accurate and stylish landing.
They were on the pharaoh's highest pyramid,
laughing and roaring so loud they started to skid...

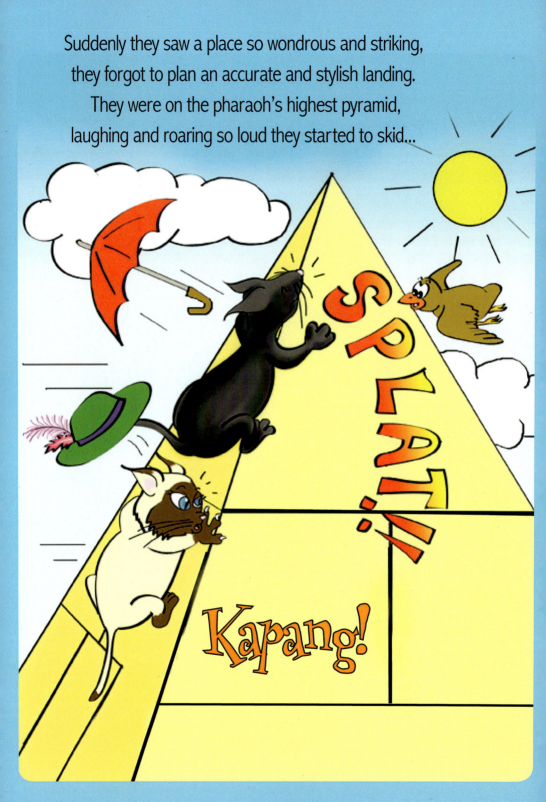

"Whey, hey!!" said Bella, hurtling fantastically fast.

"Yes! I'm going to be down first; victorious, not last!"

"WHAT!!!!!!!" called Bertie at the top of his voice,

"that's never, ever my preferred choice."

Zooming, whooshing, whooping with delight,

Bella and Bertie plummeted from the highest height.

With a thunderous splat, the cats found the soft ground.

"Yea!!!!" said Egbert. "Welcome to my home and playground!"

"Brave Bella and Bertie will you please help me out?"

"My neighbour is a mummy who always has to shout."

"His noisy bellows echo through the day and night,

giving everyone in Egypt such a terrible fright."

"Of course, Egbert we're happy to help."

"Show us the way and we'll try not to yelp."

Strolling through the kingdom of amazing beauty,

they entered the darkest pyramid to complete their duty.

Seeing the visitors, the mummy had a reason to rejoice.

"Have you come to sort out my vociferous voice?"

"Yes," said Bella and Bertie through the thunderous racket.

"Because everyone in Ancient Egypt can no longer hack it."

So Bella and Bertie approached the sad-looking mummy,

trying to look kind, friendly and funny.

Peering at each side of their new pal's head,

Bella and Bertie examined his interesting thread.

"Oh!" said Bertie. "Your bandage is over your ear."

"It's no wonder you can't hear you're shouting. Oh no! Oh dear!"

Fixing the bandage, the peculiar problem was sorted,

without their play day being aborted.

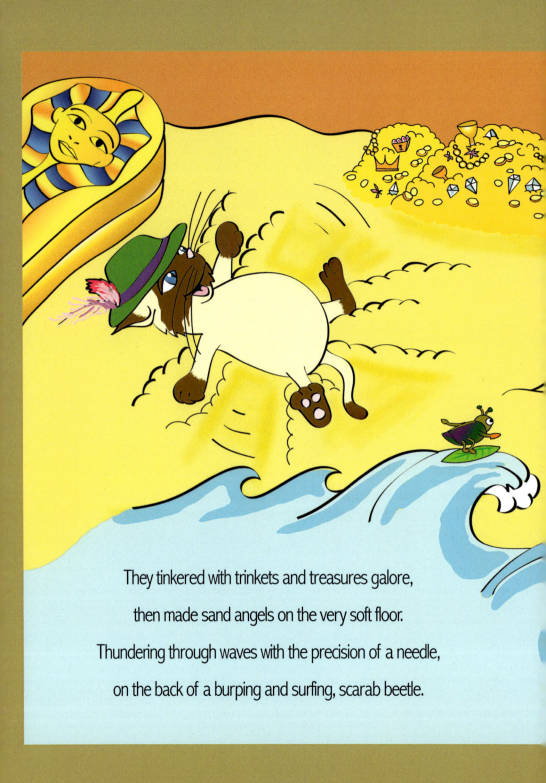

They tinkered with trinkets and treasures galore,

then made sand angels on the very soft floor.

Thundering through waves with the precision of a needle,

on the back of a burping and surfing, scarab beetle.

All day they had laughed and giggled with delight.

But, now it was late and time to say good night.

"Thank you, cousin Egbert for a super, fab stay."

"Now we must get home, before another brill day."

With their tremendous, time-travelling powers,

Bella and Bertie's laser eyes shot out like sunflowers.

They were soon galloping, clattering and scooting.

The moon's bright light, ensuring their safe commuting.

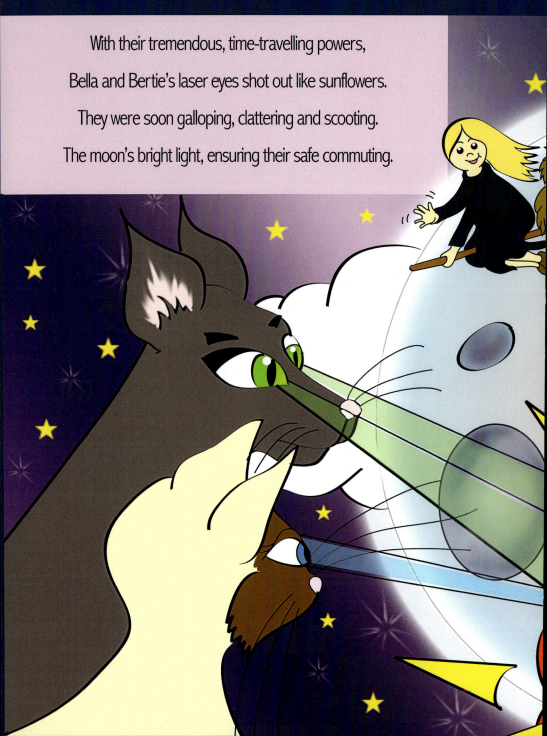

As Bella and Bertie landed safely at home,

they snuggled up in their bedtime dome.

With a drowsy, sleepy-head yawn,

Bella said, "Let's visit Enchanted Forest Fred at dawn."

Groaning, Bertie hid his head under his paws.

There's no way he'd be up before 100 snores!